THERE'S A
DRAGON
IN MY
CLOSET

WRITTEN BY

DOROTHEA TAYLOR

ILLUSTRATED BY

CHARLY PALMER

A DENENE MILLNER BOOK

BOLDEN

AN AGATE IMPRINT

CHICAGO

Printed in China

There's a Dragon in My Closet
ISBN 13: 978-1-57284-227-4
ISBN 10: 1-57284-227-X
ebook ISBN 13: 978-1-57284-806-1
ebook ISBN 10: 1-57284-806-5
First printing: August 2017

10 9 8 7 6 5 4 3 2 1   17 18 19 20 21

Bolden Books is an imprint of Agate Publishing.
Agate books are available in bulk at discount prices.
Learn more at agatepublishing.com.

For my parents, Dora and Charles Taylor, and my
grandchildren, Tirah, Noah, and Gabriel.
—DOROTHEA TAYLOR

This book is dedicated to all the image makers and dreamers out
there. Live fearlessly, love openly, give freely, and practice patience.
In return, the universe will reward you with peace and joy.
— CHARLY PALMER

There's a dragon in my closet,

there's a dragon, I swear!

I run to tell my mom and dad,

they don't believe he's there.

He's a kind and gentle dragon,

that's what I know for sure.

One day when I was sick in bed,

he left his own special cure.

While I slept, he quietly crept,

leaving candy and a letter.

He's such a con—it was signed, "Mom,"

so I wouldn't know any better.

Another day, I went out to play,

forgetting to make my bed.

I came home expecting a mess,

but found a clean room instead.

Just last week I lost a tooth,

and I don't have to be a scholar

to know it was that old dragon

who left me that crisp, new dollar.

He's mischievous, a little naughty,

of this I have the proof.

He plays in the mud in my tennis shoes,

that dragon, he's such a goof!

Once while I was brushing my teeth,

I saw him peeking through the door.

He was dancing under a sheet,

a sight that made me roar!

Panicked, my mom rushed up the stairs

to see what was the matter.

At first she thought I must have rabies,

my mouth was foaming with toothpaste lather.

"It's that silly dragon," I giggled and gagged,
"He'll do anything for a laugh."
Mommy just shook her head and sighed
and said, "Hurry up and take your bath."

He chased me 'round the living room once,

and we knocked down a flower pot.

I tried to explain to Mom and Dad,

you think they believed me? NOT!

Then there was "the cookie incident,"

I swear I only wanted one.

But that greedy dragon ate the entire jar!

And Mommy? Well, she was DONE.

"We'll get to the bottom of this," she said,

"I mean it, once and for all."

She headed toward my bedroom,

rushing swiftly down the hall.

She was a mom on a mission,

she seemed almost in a rage.

Excitement is bad for dragons,

not to mention a person her age!

She flung open my closet door,

looking quite frantic, I recall,

when out from all the clutter

bounced a lone red rubber ball.

"See, I told you, Mom," I quickly said,

"The dragon wants to play catch."

The ball was followed by a shoe, some toys,

and my pants with the big, blue patch.

As she parted my clothes hanging on the bar,
I felt myself get weak and pale.
Right there was a boot on top of my bat
and on my shoe tree, a belt for a tail.

"This closet would give me bad dreams, too,
of monsters and goblins I'd dread.
You just imagined that dragon, son,
he only exists inside your head."

That was a setup, a decoy, for sure,

planted by the dragon for my mother.

I have learned one great, big lesson,

if I have learned no other.

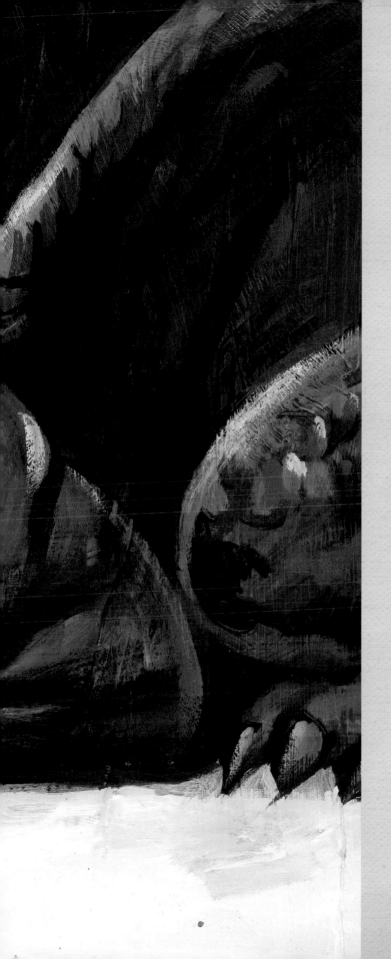

I'll never tell on the dragon,
he remains my secret friend.
Honoring that unspoken code,
he's with me through thick and thin.